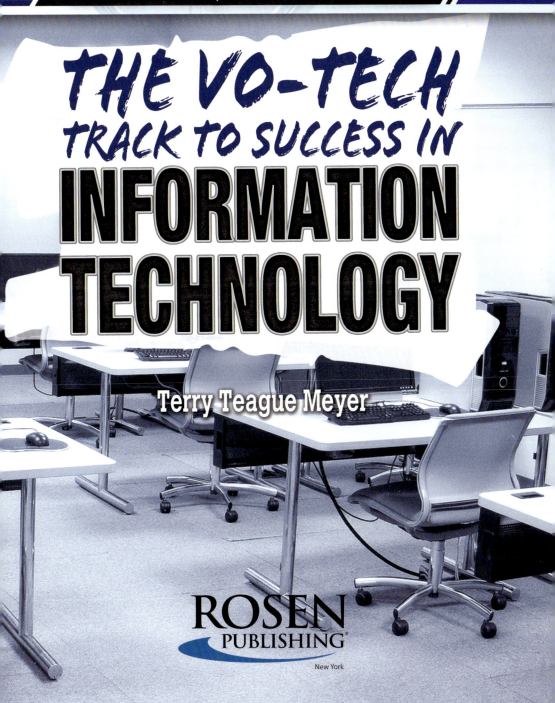

LEARNING A TRADE, PREPARING FOR A CAREER™

THE VO-TECH TRACK TO SUCCESS IN INFORMATION TECHNOLOGY

Terry Teague Meyer

ROSEN PUBLISHING
New York

Published in 2015 by The Rosen Publishing Group, Inc.
29 East 21st Street, New York, NY 10010

Copyright © 2015 by The Rosen Publishing Group, Inc.

First Edition

All rights reserved. No part of this book may be reproduced in any form without permission in writing from the publisher, except by a reviewer.

Library of Congress Cataloging-in-Publication Data

Meyer, Terry Teague, author.
The vo-tech track to success in information technology/Terry Teague Meyer.—First edition.
    pages cm.—(Learning a trade, preparing for a career)
Audience: Grades 7 to 12.
Includes bibliographical references and index.
ISBN 978-1-4777-7724-4 (library bound)
1. Computer science—Vocational guidance—Juvenile literature.
2. Information technology—Vocational guidance—Juvenile literature.
I. Title.
QA76.25.M49 2015
004.023—dc23

                                                            2013044301

Manufactured in the United States of America

CONTENTS

Introduction	4
Chapter One: **The Life and Times of an Information Technician**	7
Chapter Two: **Getting Started**	17
Chapter Three: **Specialized Training**	26
Chapter Four: **What Happens After High School?**	39
Chapter Five: **Other Considerations**	51
Glossary	66
For More Information	68
For Further Reading	71
Bibliography	73
Index	77

INTRODUCTION

Where would we be without computers and other digital devices? Computers gather, store, and process information, making it possible for people and machines to communicate with each other. They keep power plants humming and businesses working. Today's young people have grown up using them, and they (like everyone else) are likely to become more and more attached to these devices as new gadgets and applications, or apps, appear.

Taking this train of thought one step further, where would we be without information technology experts? These are the people who keep computers and networks working correctly. The term "information technology," abbreviated as "IT," covers a wide range of jobs and activities. In mid-2013, the online job resource O*NET listed 735 career areas related to information technology. It is obvious that IT training can open up many possibilities for job seekers everywhere.

Vocational training, conducted in high school or after graduation, offers a direct path to an IT career. Although many IT positions require a four-year college degree or even an advanced graduate degree, other positions are within reach through focused vocational training and certification. Taking this path is a great choice for someone who loves computers but cannot afford (or just doesn't want) to spend four years in college.

INTRODUCTION | 5

Information technology experts are needed in business, government, and education. Society depends on IT workers because everyone needs reliable computer and network services.

A vo-tech (vocational-technical) path to an IT career can start in middle school with math courses to build a strong foundation in computer basics. Working with school counselors, a high school student can plan a schedule to take full advantage of the computer training offered at his or her school. In many school districts today, students are able to take dual-credit courses, offered through community colleges, which allow them to earn college credit while working toward professional certification even before high school graduation. In some areas, work-study or internship programs offer another means to gain valuable work experience while in high school.

Beyond high school, community colleges and private technical and vocational schools offer direct paths to IT certification and employment. The federal government may help pay for this type of education or at least offer direction toward finding student financial aid. Once on the job, IT rookies may be able to further their education while working. Many companies pay for classes related to workers' jobs. Continuing education is important for IT workers because the field is always changing, with new improvements and software arriving on the scene frequently.

Information technology is a growing field and a good fit for someone who likes working with computers. But there is a lot to learn about becoming an information technician. How do IT specialists typically spend the workday? What aptitudes (natural abilities) and skills are important in this field? This book answers these questions and explores the types of high school and postsecondary (after high school) programs available. Read on for information about resources that can help students map out and follow the vo-tech track to success in information technology.

Chapter One

THE LIFE AND TIMES OF AN INFORMATION TECHNICIAN

Anyone who has ever worked with a computer or other digital device knows how unhappy users become when things don't work. Users want to know if there is a problem with the hardware or the software, or maybe with the Internet service provider, or if they've done something wrong themselves. Solving these issues and answering questions are the jobs of information technicians, who are also referred to as computer support specialists or simply IT people.

The Information Technology Association of American (ITAA) defines its members' work as "the study, design, development, implementation, support, or management of computer-based information systems, particularly software applications and computer hardware." That covers a lot! Basically, information technicians keep computers and computer networks running properly. They also do whatever is needed to help people understand how to use these technologies correctly.

"What's the Problem?"

This is a question that IT experts ask all day long. They may be asking those who call or send them e-mail messages describing computer difficulties, or they may be asking themselves as they try to figure out the cause of—and solution to—a problem. Computer problems usually take one of three forms: hardware, software, or security.

The computers and other digital devices that can be seen, touched, and turned on and off are referred to as computer hardware. IT people are called on to find and fix problems such as internal cooling fans failing, which causes them to overheat, or moisture and electrical surges that damage equipment. As with just about everything else on the planet, computer hardware simply wears out over time. Technicians also order new parts to replace those that no longer function because of age and wear.

THE LIFE AND TIMES OF AN INFORMATION TECHNICIAN | 9

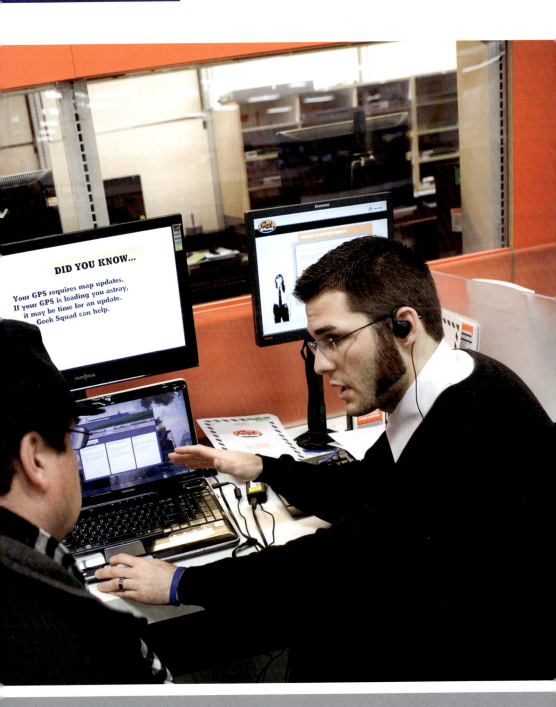

A Geek Squad technician *(right)* from Pennsylvania discusses a repair with the computer's owner. IT experts are trained to recognize whether a computer problem comes from hardware or software.

Software is the program or combination of programs designed to give instructions (in computer language) to operate a computer or other digital device. Systems software is what runs in the background to support the applications software. Examples of applications software are web browsers, games, and word processing—the tasks that most people rely on their computers to perform. Software problems can arise in the systems software or an application. Since these two types of software work together, finding the source of a problem can present a real challenge. Another issue involves software that is frequently updated. Problems can occur in a network with many users if even a few people do not have the latest version of software being used throughout. Also, when something goes wrong in a network, the difficulty in finding the source of the problem multiplies.

Computer security is another issue for IT people. Hackers breaking into computer systems to steal data or just create chaos is a growing problem. Larger companies hire specialists or bring in outside consultants just to keep their systems and networks safe. IT workers need to be trained to recognize when problems are coming from a virus or other form of computer malware (malicious software).

In addition to these three areas, problems can also be caused by the person who is trying to use a computer. Users may know little to nothing about hardware or software, or they may think they know more about those items than they really do. Problems are bound to arise from either of these scenarios. IT workers have

Computer security is an important concern. IT workers must be on the alert for hackers who try to break into computers and networks to steal data or disable systems.

to diagnose problems based on what someone else—perhaps someone with no experience—is telling them. This means that IT workers must often be mind readers of sorts, able to fix something they cannot see or touch by guiding the user through a series of tests and possible solutions.

12 | THE VO-TECH TRACK TO SUCCESS IN INFORMATION TECHNOLOGY

A Google technician works in the company's Dalles, Oregon, data center. Large companies and institutions require an army of tech people to keep things running.

Where and How They Work

IT experts are needed to set up computer systems as well as to troubleshoot. Although many individual computer users are able to set up their own systems, businesses need IT experts to install complicated networks of computers and printers, as well as provide connections for Internet service and data storage.

The term "IT" does not apply to just one type of job. As such, where an IT person works can be as varied as the type of work he or she does. Although most IT people are busy solving computer problems, the kind of company a person works for also determines how he or she spends the workday. The person who works for a large company or network to keep its operation running will have a different work experience from someone who staffs a help desk talking to individuals about computer problems.

ONE COMPANY, SEVERAL WORK ENVIRONMENTS

It is easy to imagine how many IT people a national retailer would need. Every checkout station means another computer attached to the network. Each clerk who checks to see if a product is available needs information from the system. In addition to the actual stores involved, most retailers today conduct a large amount of business through the Internet, requiring IT experts to help maintain a website.

Edward Edgerton, who has worked in IT for many years, works for a large national retailer with stores throughout the United States. He specializes in the computer applications used to forecast sales, which allows the company to order products and distribute them to stores all over the country. Edgerton is among more than one thousand IT workers employed by his company. Ninety percent of the company's IT employees, including Edgerton, work at the company's home office, where they maintain a vast computer network. Many other IT employees in his company work in two large data centers.

One Day, Lots of Jobs

The day-to-day activities of an IT worker depend on the size of the business and the number of IT workers it employs. Those who support an individual business can become familiar with the company's computer hardware, software, system, and even the users they work with every day.

For instance, take the case of a publishing company with 150 employees that employs a three-person IT team. One worker mainly handles problems with outages (failures) in the network, software updates, and system maintenance. The company's websites are created and maintained by another department within the company. The two other IT team members spend most of their time solving problems for desktop users in the main office and around the country. Most communications are done through e-mail, although urgent problems (or e-mail issues) are handled over the phone.

   As with more and more businesses these days, many of the company's employees work from home, meaning it's essential that their computers and the network are working properly. When people who work from home fail to keep their software updated, they create problems for themselves and others.

   Other IT people deal mainly with the public. Companies that need computer IT support but can't afford to create a special department within the company may get help from an outsourced help desk. Such outfits provide service to a variety of companies, meaning that the IT workers have to be familiar with a wider range of equipment and problems. Think how varied the workday would be for someone working at a help desk serving five different companies, each of them with a different hardware setup and Internet service provider and two of them with different software! But this might be the ideal job for someone who loves a challenge and doesn't like to do the same thing every day.

   Mike Whalen, who worked for such a help desk, says it is a very stressful place to work. Those calling

THE VO-TECH TRACK TO SUCCESS IN INFORMATION TECHNOLOGY

This is a view of a computer call center based in the Phillipines. IT professionals who work in such facilities must be knowledgeable in a wide variety of systems and equipment.

in are often angry and upset with their computers. It could be difficult to solve callers' problems since the help desk was a sort of middleman between the user and the company that hired them. Whalen is much happier in his current job, where he works with one other IT person handling a relatively small number of business clients. He likes the fact that he has a relationship with the people he helps.

Chapter Two

GETTING STARTED

An interest in computers is not the only reason to pursue work in the field. A career in IT—or any field, for that matter—often starts with figuring out if a person has the right skills and personality necessary for success at a particular type of job. What skills, aptitudes (natural abilities), and interests would make someone likely to succeed in an IT career? Problem solving is the main task of the IT worker. Problem solving is a skill that requires the ability to concentrate on a single issue and use deductive reasoning, which means looking at what is known to come to a reasonable conclusion. For example, if an IT worker learns that a computer user is able to send and receive e-mail and browse the Internet but is unable to create or save documents, he or she can deduce that the problem may have something to do with the word processing program.

IT problem solving requires thinking in a logical and orderly way. This is why computer help desk people usually ask about basic things first. Is the computer plugged in? Are any cables or connectors loose? Has the user tried restarting it? In this way, the IT person can rule out common user errors or see if rebooting the device will get it running properly before going further.

Teaching Someone How to Fly the Plane

Movies often show scenes of an inexperienced person having to carry out a difficult task while the expert talks him or her through it. For example, the flight attendant lands the plane or the rookie cop delivers the baby. Life can be like that for IT support people. Because IT workers often have to solve problems based on e-mail messages or phone calls, they are charged with fixing an unseen device without ever touching a switch or circuit themselves. The expert IT person is guiding someone else toward fixing a computer problem, based on information about what is wrong from someone who doesn't know how to fix it.

Communication skills are essential for someone considering a career in this field. IT support people must know how to ask questions to get the information that lets them figure out what the problem is. They must also listen carefully to the description of the problem, which means being a good listener. Considering that a caller may be upset and angry before calling for help, patience and a calm, polite manner are also essential.

In addition to listening skills and "people skills," an IT support person needs to be able to organize information and write clear, easy-to-understand explanations. Most students have written many how-to essays. How well one

Solving problems they can't see means that IT workers must have good communication skills—listening, asking the right questions, and explaining solutions in simple terms.

does with this kind of writing might indicate a promising future as an IT support person—or a need to improve one's writing skills.

Some information technicians spend time setting up computers, networks, and related equipment such as printers. Others troubleshoot and repair computer hardware. Someone who likes making models or tinkering with devices to see how they work would be happy in this part of IT work.

Plan Ahead to Get Ahead

Let's face it, many people in the computer field are college graduates, and many have advanced degrees. Being successful without a college or advanced degree requires advanced planning. Vocational training makes sense for many reasons, not the least of which is money concerns. Going to college is expensive, and some people may not be able to afford getting a four-year degree. Many students who graduate with bachelor's degrees after four years of college end up with so much student debt that they are limited in what jobs they can take and where they can live. Vo-tech programs can get people out into the workforce sooner, which allows them to start earning. Once on the job, an employer may pay for all or part of continuing education.

Middle school is a good place to start planning a vo-tech track to an IT job. As the use of technology becomes more common to complete coursework, many schools offer introductory computer classes in middle school. Students whose schools do not offer computer classes can still look to the future by mapping out a

Ohio fourth graders get a head start with computers. Taking math and (of course) computer classes early on will help prepare students for more advanced training in high school and beyond.

vo-tech path to an IT career. This could include taking math classes—computing involves a lot of math—or even courses that emphasize those all-important communication and people skills.

Seek Counseling

High school students might start planning their IT career path by discussing their interest in this type of job with a school counselor. Counselors have information about test results that can reveal a person's talents and interests. They can also help students plan for college or provide information on vocational training and work-study programs in the area.

One of the most important ways counselors can help is to put things in perspective and help students fit training into their schedules. High school course requirements to graduate vary from state to state and from one school district to another. A large number of required courses means fewer slots in a student's schedule are available for vocational

These college students are participating in a "cyberathletics" computer competition. Clubs and competitions can help increase skills while having fun.

courses. It is important to find out early how much room one's schedule will allow for gaining practical skills and experience in computer-related activities. Often courses must be taken in a certain order, and more advanced courses may not be offered every semester. In small schools or districts, it may be necessary to make a formal request, months or a year in advance, for a certain course to be offered. Counselors can help a student arrange a class schedule that makes all this work to his or her advantage.

JOIN THE CLUB

Because of possible scheduling problems, vocational courses may limit one's ability to participate in school team sports, band, or drill teams. On the other hand, school clubs and interest groups (like math and computer clubs) can help students learn outside the classroom. These same interest groups can get computer enthusiasts involved in competitions with similar groups from other schools. Participating in clubs and competitions is a fun way to meet others with shared interests and may lead to internships or financial aid.

Need Help? Look Online

Many online resources can help a young person start early on a career path. Several federal departments and agencies offer tools and information that can be accessed at home or in the public library. The U.S. Department of Labor's *Occupational Outlook Handbook* (http://www.bls.gov/ooh) includes information about salaries, outlook (number of jobs that will likely be available), and educational requirements for jobs in all areas. The handbook is updated every two years to provide reliable, current information.

O*NET (http://www.onetonline.org), another government site, lets users find out which jobs are growing and which are likely to need fewer workers in the future. The O*NET database is filled with career exploration tools and helpful resources for planning a career path, including O*NET Academy, which offers webinars, and "My Next Move," featuring an interactive tool that can help students match their interests and abilities with those related to various careers. By ranking one's preferences in sixty work-related activities, the tool creates a kind of interest profile, matching users with career possibilities based on their interests. By clicking on a given career, one finds details including salary, outlook for growth, and education and experience requirements.

The U.S. Department of Education website (http://www.ed.gov) has information on how to fund postsecondary (after high school) education through grants and loans. The same department also has information about internships and school

O*Net is an excellent career-planning resource. The site has tools to help match interests with likely careers, including many in the IT field.

accreditation agencies. Such agencies evaluate the qualifications of a school to ensure it provides the standard of education it should.

Because vo-tech education varies so much from state to state, students should be sure to check out state education and employment department websites as well. These sites offer information on specialized academies and work-study programs where students live. School district websites should also include specific graduation requirements and details on course offerings.

Chapter Three

SPECIALIZED TRAINING

The use of technology in the classroom is trying to keep up with the spread of digital devices and the importance of the Internet in people's daily lives. Computer literacy is as important to today's young people as basic math and reading skills. Large high schools in urban areas may offer a great variety of computer courses, while smaller schools and districts may have to go outside school walls to offer the variety and depth of high school courses needed to prepare someone for an IT career.

While budget limitations keep some schools from providing the latest technical resources and expertise for their students, many schools in the United States have gone high tech, providing computers and tablets for younger students and using the Internet as a resource to bring the world into the classroom. Specialized high school and middle school programs are available to train students in IT and, in some cases, give them the opportunity to earn valuable certification that attests to their knowledge in the field.

A Model Example

Several models exist that show how today's high schools can help students get on the fast track to IT jobs. Among them is Cypress-Fairbanks Independent School District (also called CyFair), a large district serving a Houston, Texas, suburban area. Computer technology courses are offered widely at the eleven high school campuses in the district, which in 2013 served a student population of more than one hundred thousand (kindergarten through high school).

The district offers several information technology courses, although not all classes are offered at every school. Courses range from basic computer programming (a prerequisite for several other courses) to advanced placement computer science. Of particular interest is a course in the essentials of telecommunications and networking, which introduces students to the basics of computer hardware and software. Students learn to assemble a computer system, install an operating system, and troubleshoot issues that might arise. They also learn about preventative maintenance, to help keep problems from occurring. Networking and security—which involves protecting computers from viruses and other malicious software, as well as keeping data safe from hackers—are also covered in these courses. A course in internetworking technologies prepares students to install, operate, and troubleshoot within a home or small business network; a follow-up course prepares students to handle the same problems for a medium-sized business branch network.

HELP! I'M NOT A GENIUS!

Many special programs are designed to find exceptionally bright and talented young people. For the average student, establishing a work history or volunteering helps to build a résumé that can lead to finding internships, financial aid for continuing education, and that first job.

A part-time job doesn't have to relate to one's chosen career to be helpful in leading to other opportunities. Any work experience is a plus on one's résumé. To a prospective employer, work history shows that a young person has a proven record of responsibility and workplace experience.

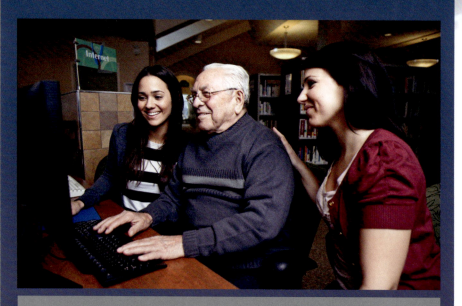

Helping seniors and other community members to use a computer is not only nice, but it also looks good on a future IT person's résumé.

SPECIALIZED TRAINING | 29

Someone who likes working with computers can be very popular! Consider volunteering at school through a peer tutoring program to help others who lack computer skills. Off campus, volunteers are often needed to teach classes in computer basics at public libraries and community and senior citizen centers. Teaching something is a great way to polish communication and presentation skills, which are important to success as an information technician.

Working with other students in school clubs and competitions is another way to demonstrate important personal skills and add to one's résumé. Assuming your schedule allows the time, consider participating in computer, math, and business clubs and projects.

Focused on helping students to become more marketable in the workplace, these courses are aligned with the exams required for industry certification. Additional courses leading to various Microsoft certifications are available through the business information management program. However, in order to complete such certifications, students must be enrolled in a dual-credit program through a local community college.

Dual-Credit Courses

As in the CyFair district, many school districts take advantage of the resources found at nearby community colleges and other postsecondary schools to offer students a chance to earn college credit before graduating from high school. CyFair is one of more than a dozen school districts in a large area surrounding Houston that have arrangements with the Lone Star College System for students to take classes for dual credit, meaning they get both high school and college credit. Lone Star is able to serve such a large area because it has seven campuses across the state.

The specifics of how dual-credit courses work depend on agreements made between a high school

Lone Star College offers students in Texas's Cypress-Fairbanks school district the chance to earn college credit for IT classes taken while they are still in high school.

or school district and the postsecondary school. Those specific arrangements determine whether the college credit would be recognized only at the school where the work was done or be transferable to another college.

Dual-credit courses typically are open only to students who demonstrate they are able to handle college-level work. Students must prove they are capable, usually by taking a preliminary test, in order to take such courses. College tuition fees may apply. Once again, a school

Students attend class at Pathways in Technology, a model tech program in Brooklyn, New York. P-Tech students receive advance tech training while in high school.

counselor would be the best person to talk to about taking these courses.

The availability of and setup for earning dual-course credit varies widely from one area to the next. According to an article on the *Northwest Florida Daily News* (Fort Walton Beach) website, students at every middle school and high school in the Okaloosa County schools can enroll in IT classes. As early as seventh and eighth grade, students can take an introduction to information technology course. After completion of that course, they are then challenged by taking Microsoft Office industry certification exams for Word, Excel, and PowerPoint. Those students who pass the introductory class earn high school credit, and those who pass the industry certification earn college credit. It should come as no surprise that these classes are very popular with students. In the Okaloosa County school district, 73 percent of the students at one middle school signed up for IT classes.

Blazing a "Pathway"

Founded in 2011, Pathways in Technology Early College High School in Brooklyn, New York, is becoming a model for a new direction in vocational education. P-Tech, as it is called, combines high school and college programs of study into a six-year program tailored for a job in the technology industry. According to an article in the *New York Times*, tech giant IBM helped develop the course of study and train the teachers. In addition, each student is paired with an IBM mentor.

Because of the large number of applicants, students at P-Tech are chosen by lottery. They attend classes from 8:35 AM to 4:06 PM in ten-period days, combining classes in traditional subjects such as math and English with those focused on technology and business. Students are taught skills such as networking, critical thinking, and how to make a good business presentation.

P-Tech has gained the attention of educators around the country. Officials in Chicago have opened similar schools with corporate partners in telecommunications and technology. Other states—including Maine, Massachusetts, Missouri, North Carolina, and Tennessee—have plans for similar schools in the works.

Members of the Academy

Some of the most exciting vo-tech training takes place in specialized learning academies that bring together students to focus on skills and knowledge needed for certain careers and career clusters. While many such career academies are housed inside classrooms and buildings on school grounds, students might have to take a specialized course at a different location off-campus either during school hours or outside regular school hours. Many career academies benefit from the support of business partners who provide students with mentoring and work-study opportunities.

Career academies provide students with a college-level curriculum that focuses on career preparedness.

34 | THE VO-TECH TRACK TO SUCCESS IN INFORMATION TECHNOLOGY

A skeleton advertises science and tech academy offerings during a Florida middle school district open house. Many school districts are creating academies to provide advanced training in these career fields.

SPECIALIZED TRAINING | 35

These academic organizations encourage students to work together, focusing on a theme or project while also emphasizing a different core course like English or math each year. Students must apply to be admitted to an academy, and acceptance may be determined by factors such as academic performance, attendance, and conduct.

According to an article in *T.H.E. (Technology Horizons in Education) Journal*, the career academy concept began in one area of Florida as an economic development tool to keep local young people from leaving the area after graduation. The Academy of Information Technology and Robotics (AITR) in the Volusia County (Florida) school district is one of a number of career academies in the Volusia County system. Housed in Spruce Creek High School in Port Orange, Florida, the program has strong local support from the community in the form of finances and mentoring. Spruce Creek serves 2,900 students, about 800 of whom come from different school districts to take classes at the academy.

A wide variety of computer courses are offered at AITR. A hardware track includes an introductory course and three follow-up classes in PC support, while the software track offers ten different courses. There are more course offerings under the gaming simulation and robotics tracks. In addition, Spruce Creek High School itself offers computer courses with a business technology focus. The student experience also includes field studies, career shadowing (observing workers in the chosen career during the workday), and internships. There is even a business partner group called the Career Connection Cadre.

The National Academy Foundation (NAF) launched Academies of Information Technology (AOIT) in twelve high schools in 2000, with support from a number of corporate sponsors in the field of technology. According to the NAF website, in the 2011–2012 school year, 105 such academies served almost 16,000 students in 60 different school districts across the country. The majority are minority/economically disadvantaged students.

NAF-sponsored academies not only teach students IT skills but also provide information useful in getting a good job. For example, students learn how to write a résumé and how to perform well in a job interview. NAF schools get help from local and national companies

SPECIALIZED TRAINING | **37**

THE STUDENT-BUSINESS CONNECTION

In 2011, Harvard University Graduate School of Education published "Pathways to Prosperity," a report focused on the need for improved vocational training through partnerships between schools and businesses. Students need the opportunity to learn not only in the classroom but also through work experience in their chosen field. Businesses benefit from such partnerships as the pool of workers qualified to fill jobs requiring technical expertise grows. The report cites the career academy movement and a number of similar programs as models for the future of vo-tech. Among other examples are High Schools That Work, developed by the Southern Regional Education Board, and the Linked Learning Initiative in California.

that offer advice, mentoring, and summer internships for students.

The NAF sponsors academies in career areas other than IT. All such academies are part of their local school districts. There is no cost to students, who gain entry into an academy through their district's regular school choice process. Some academies are schools within larger public high schools, and some are stand-alone small schools. A few others are charter schools. Most of these academies are clustered in urban areas, but there are some in suburban and rural areas as well.

IT Training Goes Mainstream

Students in many high school vocational training areas such as auto repair, agriculture, and cosmetology can be isolated from the general high school population by classroom location or emphasis of study. The situation is somewhat different in the area of computers and information technology. Some degree of computer literacy is now considered an essential skill for all high school graduates, not just those on the IT vo-tech career path. High school students in basic computer courses—and many advanced ones—may be planning to use computer knowledge in careers in business or design. Still others may be preparing to study computer science in college. Students planning to work in the IT field as soon as possible after high school take classes with students planning to earn four-year or advanced degrees in computer science, engineering, or other areas of science and technology. High school IT courses may be challenging, but the rewards are great in terms of useful knowledge—whether that knowledge is used for college or career.

Chapter Four

WHAT HAPPENS AFTER HIGH SCHOOL?

As more and more people attend college, businesses are becoming choosier about hiring and generally favor those with some education beyond the high school diploma. Continuing one's education beyond high school can definitely put one on the fast track to an IT job and open up more career paths.

Students can receive IT education after high school at a variety of places: community colleges, private for-profit vocational schools (also known as career colleges), and organizations that offer courses geared toward certification. Another choice to be made is whether to attend classes in person or take courses online. Which way students go depends on how much money and time they can afford to spend. Other factors to consider include learning style and level of self-discipline.

Welcome to the Community

Community colleges, as the name suggests, are local institutions supported in part by local or state tax funds.

Tax-payer support means less tuition cost for the student. In large metropolitan areas, there may be several community colleges or different campuses with varying course offerings. Considering the growing importance of computers, it should not be hard to find IT courses.

Community colleges and many career colleges offer associate's degrees, which are awarded based on a two-year program of study. An associate's degree program requires students to take certain core courses that don't relate to IT. This means that students working toward an associate's degree have to take—and pay for—courses other than those pertaining to their IT career path. Students end up with a degree, and having a degree is often the key to a higher salary.

When choosing a community college, the student should map out a possible future course. Is it possible to earn a two-year associate's degree in one's vocational area? Is it best to take courses leading directly to specific computer certifications? What is the best way to use dual credits earned in high school? These are questions the student should discuss with a high school counselor after studying the course offerings

and figuring out short- and long-term goals. Students thinking of continuing their education and working toward a four-year college degree should also investigate which schools accept community or career college courses toward a four-year degree. Whether

Mass Bay Community College students work together while taking a computer class in Massachusetts. Community colleges offer two-year degrees.

or not credit can be transferred depends on agreements between the schools involved.

Community college and state programs are not free. Some students have to schedule classes around a full-time job to be able to continue vocational training after high school. If the need to work means the student will be taking classes over a long period of time, it's important to know whether or not there is a time limit for completing a degree program. As in high school, it may be difficult for those taking one or two classes at a time to sign up for required courses in the proper order. For working students, online training is a good option because of its flexibility. On the other hand, the student may need the structure of a class with other learners and the help of a teacher he or she can talk to.

Certainly Certifiable

According to a June 2012 study conducted by the Georgetown University Center on Education and the Workforce, postsecondary certificates are the second most popular postsecondary award; the bachelor's degree is first. Certification programs are often the fastest, most cost-effective way to increase one's earning power.

There are many different kinds of certification programs. The Georgetown report refers specifically to certificates awarded by schools based on time spent in the classroom. Over a million such certificates were awarded in 2010.

Postsecondary certificate programs vary in length, purpose, and location. Some programs take less than a year to complete, while others take from one to two years. The rewards are worth whatever the wait. A 2000 National Education Longitudinal study has shown that students who earn certificates and begin careers in areas such as IT earn up to 40 percent more than high school graduates.

These Florida high school students are taking advanced training that will earn them valuable IT certifications. Earning recognized certification makes it easier to find work in the field.

The quickest way to get certified might not include school credits that can be used toward an eventual degree. For example, Texas's Lone Star College System has different courses for credit and noncredit students. The noncredit path, referred to as the system's "fast track," is for students who wish to learn a skill quickly but are not concerned with earning credit that could be transferred to another school.

A second kind of certification is based on taking exams related to specific computer-industry products. A 2010 article in *PCWorld* titled "IT Certifications That Matter" offers advice to companies planning to hire certified job candidates. Within the article, certificates

IN SEARCH OF A CERTIFICATION PROGRAM

An online search of computer certifications leads to many lists of certifications with links to study guides, exam centers, and courses to prepare for the exams. Some certifications are for people already at work in the industry. Others are being taken by middle school and high school students around the country. Many high school and postsecondary classes focus on preparing students to pass these certification exams. There are also online and short classroom courses available to prepare for them.

Because computer technology is constantly changing, it would be a good idea to discuss the most useful certifications and the best way to prepare for them with a school computer instructor.

are divided into groups. Some certifications focus on certain brands of equipment and software such as Apple or Microsoft. According to the article, the basic Cisco Certified Network Associate (CCNA) certification is among the most popular in the industry. The non-profit Computing Technology Industry Association (CompTIA) offers certification not specific to any product. This certification would be good to have, as it would show that an IT job candidate is qualified to work with more than one type of computer hardware and software.

The Electronics Technicians Association (ETA International), a nonprofit professional organization, also offers certifications. The ETA website includes a detailed list of the knowledge and competencies (ability to do something efficiently and successfully) needed to become a certified network computer technician. This list could be used as a self-check to track one's computer knowledge as it increases.

Vocational and Trade Schools

Whether they realize it or not, most people are not far from a campus of a for-profit vocational or trade school. One can easily locate such a school by doing an online search for "vocational training" or "IT education." These schools offer either classroom or online training or both types of instruction. Community colleges are supported in part by taxpayer contributions, so tuition is often lower than at for-profit schools. On the other hand, some for-profit vocational schools have a more narrow focus and can provide the skills one needs to get a job more quickly.

ONE PERSON'S EXPERIENCE

Ted Mahaney has been working in the IT field for fifteen years since completing a ten-month program (approximately fifteen hours a week) with the Computer Learning Center in Houston. His training was concentrated on computer networking, specifically Novell and Microsoft Windows certification training. Although the school did not offer him direct assistance in getting a job, Mahaney feels that the computer training he received helped him get his foot in the workplace door. In fact, he was able to find an IT position even before he completed his training. He currently works as a senior network administrator.

"Don't wait for anyone to find you a job," Mahaney advises. "As soon as you feel you have some skills, get out there and look so you can get an entry-level position." He also mentions that finding a mentor is a real plus in career advancement.

Finding a Good Value

It is important to research all options before investing time and money in a vocational or trade program. It is a good idea to learn all you can about the school even before making a campus visit. Once again, a high school counselor may be able to provide ready information. The next place to visit is the school's website. After all, any institution with a good IT program should have a user-friendly website.

Websites describing schools and programs are required to make detailed statements and explanations as to requirements for enrolling students. The first place students should look is any web page labeled "important consumer information" or with similar language. Look for answers to these questions on the

A high school counselor *(right)* talks to a student and her mother in New Jersey. Counselors and teachers can help students find a good postsecondary program.

website: Is the school accredited? How long will the program take? Can a student take certain courses toward certification or must he or she commit to a set program or degree? Information on how much an education at a specific institution is going to cost may be found at a link on the school's website labeled "net price calculator." This tool helps a student figure out the actual cost associated with various programs.

By exploring the catalog of classes, you should be able to find out whether the school offers courses toward certification or only straightforward degree plans. Before signing up for a program, be sure you understand the actual costs and any terms related to completing the program.

In Class or Online

Students pursuing a career in the IT field have the option of taking instruction in a classroom or via the Internet. By taking online courses, students may find educational facilities and programs that fit their needs better than what is available close by.

The Tennessee Technology Centers offer an excellent model for vocational training. There are twenty-seven technology centers around the state, and courses are available to out-of-state students online. Tennessee Technology Centers allow students to work at their own pace so that advancement through a program is based on the individual's mastery of skills. However, interaction between students and instructors is also part of what makes TTC

LET THE BUYER BEWARE

Disturbed by the number of students dropping out of programs after taking out loans to pay for expensive tuition, the federal government began looking into some of the practices of for-profit schools. This research uncovered some alarming patterns. The Government Accountability Office (GAO) issued a report to Congress in August 2010 including the results of an undercover investigation into practices among for-profit schools. (Note that these reports cover a wide range of vocational training—not only computer or IT training.) Some prospective students were encouraged to lie on forms for loan and grant applications. Some recruiters trying to enroll students lied to them about the cost of their programs compared with costs at nearby community colleges. Recruiters sometimes misled students about job prospects, help in obtaining jobs, and salaries students could expect after completing the programs.

Another report, issued in July 2012 for a U.S. Senate committee, indicated that for-profit schools charged four times as much in tuition for an associate's degree or certification as comparable not-for-profit schools. The report found a high dropout rate at such schools. A reason for the Senate committee's concern is that much of the money going to these schools is coming from loan and grant programs supported by U.S. tax dollars.

programs outstanding. It is unclear whether that interaction would be as effective for a student taking the program online.

No matter how good an online program is, it might not be the best choice for some students. When considering whether to choose a classroom setting or online program, it is important to understand your learning style. Ask yourself whether you are a self-starter who will keep up a schedule of online sessions on your own. Do you need the structure of a scheduled class time? Some students need face time with a teacher and the interaction with fellow students to help them master subject material. For these students, online training is not the best choice.

Chapter Five

OTHER CONSIDERATIONS

While not as expensive as getting a four-year or graduate degree, the vo-tech track to a career in IT can still have a financial burden attached. Students considering this career path must consider how they plan to pay for their vo-tech education. Loans can be repaid once someone has gotten a job as an IT professional—but getting that job, and hanging on to it, require some planning and effort as well.

Paying Your Way

Cost may be a factor in choosing the best place to get vocational training after high school. Figuring out how to pay for continuing education can be complicated. However, most schools provide advice through financial aid offices and counselors. Financing options include grants, loans, internships, work-study programs, or a combination of these.

Government Assistance

The federal government is a good place to start seeking information about school financing. The U.S. Department of Education's site (http://www.ed.gov) is easy to navigate, with links to information about various sources of school financing. In Canada, the CanLearn site (http://www.canlearn.ca) contains the same type of information on obtaining education financing.

A first step in seeking financial aid from the U.S. government is completing the FAFSA (Free Application for Federal Student Aid) form. This common application form is used not only by the federal government but by private institutions as well. The FAFSA asks for personal information (driver's license number, Social Security number, and much more) about the applicant and his or her family. The applicant must also report family income information taken from income tax forms. The purpose of the FASFA is to come up with the amount of money an individual and his or her family can be expected to contribute toward an education (the EFC, or expected family contribution) and then determine the difference between that amount and the projected cost of the education (the COA, or cost of attending). This gap in funding represents a prospective student's official financial need and eligibility for grants and scholarships based on need.

In addition to the federal government, states may also provide student loans. The Department of Education Student Financial Aid website has links to state financial offices and other information about loans.

OTHER CONSIDERATIONS | 53

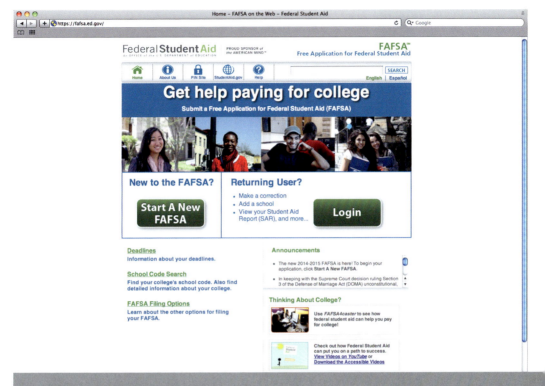

No matter where you plan to attend college or vocational school, the Federal Student Aid website (http://www.fasfa.ed.gov) is one of the best places to start looking for funding.

An Aid Primer

Not all financial aid is alike. Knowing what's what can help avoid a mountain of student debt. The most popular types of school financial aid are grants, scholarships, and loans.

Grants are money that does not need to be repaid. However, a student who receives a grant (the grantee) may be limited in how the money can be used. The grantee must also meet course and grade requirements. Grants may come from the federal government, state governments, or private organizations.

Scholarships are money for education that is usually based on academic or other achievement (like athletic or music ability). Like grants, scholarships usually don't have to be repaid. In general, the basis of getting a grant is need, while a scholarship is based on merit. Of course, many young people are both financially needy and accomplished students! Scholarships are often awarded to college students by the school that accepted them.

Scholarships are available from a number of sources. Some small scholarships are available only to certain people—certain ethnic groups, families in military service, or residents of a specific area, for example. The Federal Student Aid page on the Department of Education website has several links to help in finding scholarships, including a link to the Department of Labor's free scholarship search tool. This search tool will pull up information about available financial aid based on the type of school someone attends, the type of aid, the state where one lives, and other special limitations like gender, ethnic group, disability, and the like.

Just like a car loan, a student loan must be repaid with interest, which is cost added on to the amount borrowed. Federal student loans generally have more favorable terms than those available from banks, but these terms are subject to change based on action by Congress. The Federal Perkins Loan Program for students with exceptional financial need provides funding through schools that participate in the program. In 2013, for example, students at participating schools could borrow up to $5,500 at 5 percent annual interest. The school acts as a lender by reducing school costs to the student by the amount of the loan. Students have to begin repaying the loan nine

Applying for a college loan is much the same process as with any other kind of loan. Students should be sure that they understand the terms of any loan before applying.

months after leaving school. The Perkins Loan Program is limited in funds, and like any federal program, is subject to change in the future.

Needless to say, it is important to understand the terms of loan agreements, as repayment begins according to the loan agreement whether or not the former student has a job.

Internships and Apprenticeships—What's the Difference?

Apprenticeships have long been common in trades like carpentry and plumbing. Such an arrangement is based on an agreement between the apprentice and the worker who will do the training. This agreement covers the amount the apprentice will be paid and what he or she expects to learn over the course of the apprenticeship.

This model is used in the Wisconsin Youth Apprenticeship (YA) program. The program, which is available in about half of the state's school districts, is regarded as one of the nation's largest apprenticeship opportunities for high school students, covering many vocational areas. According to information found on the Wisconsin Department of Workforce Development website, this work-study arrangement has specific guidelines for what is expected of the student and the employer. Students are paid for the hours they work and benefit from the hands-on experience.

WORK-STUDY INFORMATION

The U.S. DOE site also has links and information about work-study programs. Many postsecondary schools participate in such programs in partnership with the federal government. The student works part-time at an hourly rate in order to pay for part of his or her education. The jobs are located either at the school or at a nonprofit or government-related agency. In general, work-study jobs off campus are related to public interest, rather than to the student's course of study.

The Wisconsin YA IT program lasts for two years. Students focus on computer basics during the first year. In the second year, youth apprentices can specialize in hardware, software, or web and digital media, according to their personal interests and where they are working. Because IT workers are needed in so many types of business, YA work sites can be chosen from any business that can train students in the required competencies.

In contrast, the term "internship" has a broader definition. The meaning of the term really depends on who is offering the internship! Because internships are frequently unpaid positions, they are not always a means to help pay for one's education. Author Ross

Perlin, in his book *Intern Nation: How to Earn Nothing and Learn Little in the Brave New Economy,* criticizes the many businesses and non-profit organizations that use unpaid interns. Perlin notes that some interns do meaningless work like delivering coffee while others do very important work and get no credit or payment in return. Those who favor internships argue that interns gain valuable experience in the workplace, even if they receive no formal training.

Paid interns are likely to be those with postsecondary training in a specific area. For example, the computer company HP offers paid summer internships to IT students who have completed their freshman year and shown high academic achievement. Paid internships at many companies are reserved for students the company would like to hire after they complete a bachelor's or advanced degree.

An information systems student checks the offerings during a Clemson University Career Fair. Colleges and vocational schools can help steer students toward not only jobs, but also internships.

There are a number of websites designed to locate and match internships with likely candidates. However, it might be most productive to look for an internship close to home. As noted in the chapter on high school programs, businesses in some communities make internships available through local schools. Students should also consider other possible sources of internships (and financial aid): a parent's place of employment, religious organizations, social and service organizations such as Scouting, and professional organizations. These businesses and organizations may have reserved internships and scholarships specifically for someone like you.

Josh's Story

Sometimes the path from interest in a career to reaching one's goal is not straight and direct. Preparing for an IT career, picking the right school, and completing a training program all involve personal choices and personal commitment. Each person's experience is as unique as the person him- or herself.

Consider the case of Josh Mann. Josh's interest in an IT career began in the eighth grade, when he visited a high school computer technology class. Later he wound up taking that same course himself, which included a two-hour block of classes each day. After high school he began taking general classes at a nearby community college, but he didn't continue for long, opting instead to enter the workforce.

After working for two years, he signed up for computer classes at ITT Tech, a for-profit technical school

YEAR UP: A BRIGHT SPOT FOR URBAN YOUTH

Since 2001, an innovative program called Year Up has offered vo-tech training and internships to young people between the ages of eighteen and twenty-four. Founded in Boston, the program now serves more than 1,900 students a year in ten urban areas. According to the Harvard "Pathways to Prosperity" report, Year Up is an outstanding model partnership between business and education. The program includes six months of classroom training in professional and technical skills, followed by placement as an intern for an additional six months. Students receive a weekly stipend throughout the program, but they can be docked money for things like showing up for class late or not completing assignments on time.

Applicants are chosen based on a number of factors, but grades are not the most important one. A candidate's work ethic and commitment to the program are also considered in the screening process. More than 250 corporate sponsors participate in the program not only to support their communities but also because they are looking for young people who are well trained and professional in manner. New participants in the nonprofit program begin each September and March.

with branches throughout the United States. ITT Tech offers both bachelor's and associate's degrees in a number of disciplines, including IT. Josh had to pay for his entire education by working full-time and getting government loans, but he was very happy with the education he received. Even though attending the school was expensive, he liked the flexibility of studying there, which made it possible for him to work while he took classes. He also found the classes more and more challenging as he continued—challenging in a good way.

Josh completed his associate's degree in two years. Although he specialized in computer courses, networking in particular, he also took general courses in communications, problem solving, and writing. After he graduated, the school helped him find a job at an insurance company IT help desk. He enjoyed the work there, but he wanted to move into a career in computer security. So while continuing to work, he went back to ITT Tech and earned a bachelor of science degree in information systems security. Josh now works as an IT administrator for a small computer security company in the Houston, Texas, area.

Josh's story shows that finding the right career path depends on the individual. His path took him from an early interest in IT through a vo-tech education, first at an associate level, then as a bachelor's degree candidate. This example also shows the importance of commitment to one's decision. Josh watched many of his fellow students drop out as classes became more challenging. Once he had decided to go back to school for the second time he stuck with it, despite having to juggle a job and increasingly difficult subject material. He didn't take a direct path from his first high school IT class to where he is now. But his persistence and focus on mastering new material paid off, to the point that he eventually earned a spot in the field that first drew his interest way back in middle school.

Minding One's Business

No matter where one gets the skills and training to prepare for a career in computers and information technology, job applicants need to know something about the business world. Young people may not have the money to buy a business suit for an interview, but they should realize how important it is to dress to project a professional appearance. Baggy pants, short skirts, frayed jeans, and flip-flops are not appropriate. It may turn out later that the workplace has a very casual atmosphere, but it is best to assume that they are seeking employees who look like business professionals, rather than students.

These days, getting an in-person interview is often a later step in the hiring process. Often a telephone interview comes first, for preliminary screening. Needless to say, the telephone interview is an important opportunity to make a good first impression. Because many IT jobs involve telephone communications, speaking clearly and politely over the phone is a particular asset. Written communications are also important in IT work, so make

A telephone interview is often the first step in the hiring process. Students trying to land an IT job might want to practice their phone skills with a friend or mentor.

sure that any communications are free of errors, slang, and casual abbreviations.

A young person's first job is very important, even if it doesn't relate directly to a chosen career path. Anyone who has shown the ability to consistently show up at work on time and carry out duties with energy and enthusiasm at a fast-food restaurant, a store, a construction site, or any other place of employment has demonstrated qualities that employers value. Don't be afraid to include high school jobs in a résumé—as long as you left the employer with a commendable record.

Young people should start thinking early about their online presence on the web. Internet photos, videos, and statements are easily accessed by prospective employers and at this point are very difficult to remove once they are online. The best way to avoid damaging your reputation and job prospects is to be careful about what you and your friends make public.

Glossary

accreditation The recognition that a school meets acceptable standards of quality. An approved outside agency will study a school to determine whether or not it can be called "accredited."

application software A computer program designed with the user in mind.

aptitude A talent or particular ability.

career college Another term for a vocational or technical school, with an emphasis on technical training for specific careers.

certification Official recognition that someone or something has certain qualifications or meets certain standards.

community college A postsecondary school that is supported in part by local public funding, typically offering two-year programs and awarding associate's degrees.

competency The ability to do something successfully; a skill.

consultant One who gives professional advice in exchange for payment.

curriculum The content of courses studied in an educational program.

dual-credit courses Courses for which a high school student can earn high school and college credit at the same time.

funding Money provided, especially by an organization or government, for a particular purpose.

grant Funds given to a person or an organization to be used for a specific purpose.

information technology (IT) Work that supports computer and other digital information systems, particularly hardware and software.

internship A period of working while training, with or without pay, to gain experience in a career field.

postsecondary education Courses or training done after one leaves high school.

prerequisite Course that must be taken before, and in preparation for, a more advanced course.

recruiter A person whose job is to enroll people in a school or group, or to join a cause.

résumé A short description of someone's education and work experience given to prospective employers when one is seeking a job.

stipend A sum of money that is paid to someone to cover their living expenses.

vocation A job or career.

For More Information

Association for Computing Machinery (ACM)
1515 Broadway
New York, NY 10036
(800) 342-6626
Website: http://www.acm.org
A professional organization supports those in the computer field and those preparing for such careers. The ACM includes student members and also sponsors student competitions.

Manitoba Office of Technical Vocational Education
1567 Dublin Avenue
Winnipeg, MB R3E 3J5
Canada
(800) 281-8069, ext. 1037
Website: http://www.edu.gov.mb.ca/tve/link.html
This office has information about technical vocational education and apprenticeships in Manitoba and links to related programs in other parts of Canada.

Ontario Ministry of Training, Colleges and Universities
14th Floor, Mowat Block
900 Bay Street
Toronto, ON M7A 1L2
Canada
(800) 387-5514
Website: http://www.information.met.ontario.ca
This office has information on employment profiles, current employment trends, and the outlook for various careers in the future. The website

includes links to information about choosing a career, finding a school or program, and funding an education.

Technology Student Association
1914 Association Drive
Reston, VA 20191-1540
(888) 860-9010
Website: http://www.tsaweb.org
The Technology Student Association is a national organization for middle school and high school students interested in technology. The association sponsors leadership and teamwork through projects and competitions.

U.S. Department of Education
400 Maryland Avenue SW
Washington, DC 20202
(800) USA-LEARN (372-5327)
Website: http://www.edu.gov
The U.S. Department of Education carries out a number of functions. It is charged with collecting data on schools, distributing federal financial aid, and ensuring equal access to education. It offers information about choosing a postsecondary school and paying for one's education.

U.S. Department of Labor
200 Constitution Avenue NW
Washington, DC 20210
(866) 487-2365

Website: http://www.dol.gov
The Department of Labor gathers statistics about jobs. The DOL sponsors a variety of websites and provides links to up-to-date information about careers, including salaries, preparation needed, and projected growth.

Websites

Due to the changing nature of Internet links, Rosen Publishing has developed an online list of websites related to the subject of this book. This site is updated regularly. Please use the following link to access the list:

http://www.rosenlinks.com/TRADE/IT

For Further Reading

Berger, Sandra L. *The Ultimate Guide to Summer Opportunities for Teens.* Waco, TX: Prufrock Press, Inc., 2009.

Chertavian, Gerald. *A Year Up: How a Pioneering Program Teaches Young Adults Real Skills for Real Jobs—with Real Success.* New York, NY: Viking, 2012.

Christian, Carol, and Richard N. Bolles. *What Color Is Your Parachute? For Teens.* 2nd ed. New York, NY: Ten Speed Press, 2010.

Farenden, Peter. *ITIL for Dummies.* Chichester, West Sussex, England: John Wiley and Sons, 2012.

Farr, Michael. *Top 100 Computer and Technical Careers: Your Complete Guidebook to Major Jobs in Many Fields at All Training Levels.* 4th ed. Indianapolis, IN: JIST Publishing, 2009.

Fireside, Bryna J. *Choices for the High School Graduate: A Survival Guide for the Information Age.* 5th edition. New York, NY: Ferguson, 2009.

Freedman, Jeri. *Careers in Computer Support.* New York, NY: Rosen Publishing, 2013.

Gerbyshak, Phil, and Jeffrey M. Brooks. *Help Desk Manager's Crash Course.* North Charleston, SC: BookSurge Publishing, 2009.

Hutchins, Heather Z. *I Don't Want to Go to College: Other Paths to Success.* Chicago, IL: Huron Press, 2013.

Llewellyn, Bronwyn A., and Robin Holt. *The Everything Career Tests Book: 10 Tests to Determine the Right Occupation for You.* Avon, MA: F+W Publications, 2007.

Lore, Nicolas. *Now What? A Young Person's Guide to Choosing the Perfect Career.* New York, NY: Touchstone Books, 2008.

Lore, Nicolas. *The Pathfinder: How to Choose or Change Your Career for a Lifetime of Satisfaction.* Revised ed. New York, NY: Touchstone Books, 2012.

McCoy, Lisa. *Computers and Programming.* New York, NY: Ferguson (Infobase Publishing), 2010.

Miller, Michael. *Absolute Beginner's Guide to Computer Basics.* 5th ed. Indianapolis, IN: Que/Pearson Education, 2010.

Price, Michael. *Computer Basics in Easy Steps.* 8th ed. Southam Warwickshire, England: Easy Steps Limited, 2011.

Reeves, Ellen Gordon. *Can I Wear My Nose Ring to the Interview?: The Crash Course. Finding, Landing, and Keeping Your First Real Job.* New York, NY: Workman Publishing, 2009.

Shelly, Gary B., and Misty E. Vermaat. *Discovering Computers—Fundamentals.* 2011 ed. Boston, MA: Course Technology, Cengage Learning, 2011.

Snyder, Thomas. *The Community College Career Track: How to Achieve the American Dream Without a Mountain of Debt.* Hokoken, NJ: Wiley, 2012.

Troy-Brooks, Patricia. *Your Job Search GPS: Navigate to Your Career Destination in 10 Steps.* Charleston, SC: Createspace, 2012.

Zichy, Shoya, and Ann Bidou. *Career Match: Connecting Who You Are with What You'll Love to Do.* New York, NY: AMACOM, 2007.

Bibliography

Baker, Al. "At Technology High School, Goal Isn't to Finish in 4 Years." *New York Times*, October 21, 2012. Retrieved August 12, 2013 (http://www.nytimes.com/2012/10/22/nyregion/pathways-in-technology-early-college-high-school-takes-a-new-approach-to-vocational-education.html?hpw&_r=1&).

Bruzzese, Anita. "Program Helps Young People Get Skills for Available Jobs." USAToday.com, April 17, 2011. Retrieved, September 2, 2013 (http://usatoday30.usatoday.com/money/jobcenter/workplace/bruzzese/2011-04-20-year-up-program-helps-with-job-skills_N.htm).

Carnevale, Anthony P., et al. "Career and Technical Education: Five Ways That Pay Along the Way to the B.A." Georgetown University Center on Education and the Workforce, September 16, 2012. Retrieved August 15, 2013 (http://www9.georgetown.edu/grad/gppi/hpi/cew/pdfs/CTE.FiveWays.FullReport.pdf).

Carnevale, Anthony P., et al. "Certificates: Gateway to Gainful Employment and College Degrees." Georgetown University Center on Education and the Workforce, June 2012. Retrieved August 17, 2013 (http://www9.georgetown.edu/grad/gppi/hpi/cew/pdfs/Certificates.FullReport.061812.pdf).

Federal Trade Commission. "Consumer Information: Choosing a Vocational School." Retrieved June 10, 2013 (http://www.consumer.ftc.gov/articles/0241-choosing-vocational-school).

Forroohar, Rana. "These Schools Mean Business: Corporations Help School U.S. Students in Technology." *Time*, April 9, 2010. Retrieved May 14, 2013 (http://content.time.com/time/magazine/article/0,9171,2110455,00.html).

Goodman, Pete S. "The New Poor: In Hard Times, Lured into Trade School and Debt." *New York Times*, March 13, 2010. Retrieved June 14, 2013 (http://www.nytimes.com/2010/03/14/business/14schools.html?pagewanted=all&_r=1&).

Grobe, Terry, et al. "Dollars and Sense: How 'Career First' Programs Like Year Up Benefit Youth and Employers." Jobs for the Future Report, May 2010. Retrieved August 23, 2013 (www.jff.org/sites/default/files DollarsSense_05251v3.pdf).

Harvard Graduate School of Education. "Pathways to Prosperity Project: Meeting the Challenge of Preparing Young Americans for the 20th Century." February 2011. Retrieved September 3, 2013 (http://www.gse.harvard.edu/news_events/features/2011/Pathways_to_Prosperity_Feb2011.pdf).

Lewin, Tamar. "Student-Loan Borrowers Average $26,500 in Debt." *New York Times*, October 18, 2012. Retrieved: May 20, 2013 (http://www.nytimes.com/2012/10/18/education/report-says-average-student-loan-debt-is-up-to-26500.html?ref=tamarlewin&_r=1&).

Mann, Joshua T., Interview with the author, September 2013.

Perlin, Ross. *Intern Nation: How to Earn Nothing and Learn Little in the Brave New Economy.* Brooklyn, NY: Verso, 2011.

Pierce, Margo. "A Community Affair in Florida." *T H E Journal* 39, no.4, 2012. Computer Source, EBSCOhost. Retrieved August 19, 2013.

Tammen, Katie. "IT Program Big Hit in Middle Schools." *Northwest Florida Daily News*, April 16, 2013. EBSCOhost. Retrieved August 19, 2013.

Taylor, Allan, and James Robert Parish. *Career Opportunities in Library and Information Science.* New York, NY: Checkmark Books, 2009.

U.S. Bureau of Labor Statistics. "Computer Support Specialists." *Occupational Outlook Handbook.* Retrieved June 20, 2013 (http://www.bls.gov/ooh/computer-and-information-technology).

U.S. Government Accountability Office. "For-Profit Colleges: Undercover Testing Finds Colleges Encouraged Fraud and Engaged in Questionable and Deceptive Marketing Practices." Retrieved May 15, 2013 (http://www.gao.gov/new.items/d10948t.pdf).

U.S. Senate Committee on Health, Education, Labor & Pensions: Newsroom–Press Release. "Harkin: Report Reveals Troubling Realities of For-Profit Schools." Retrieved July 19, 2013 (http://www.help.senate.gov/newsroom/press/release/?id=45c8ca2a-b290-47ab-b452-74d6e6bdb9dd).

Wenzel, Elsa. "IT Certifications That Matter." *PCWorld*, November 2, 2010. Retrieved

August 24, 2012 (http://www.pcworld.com/ article/209227/it_certifications_that_matter _for_helpdesk_tech_support_pros.html).

Wisconsin Department of Workforce Development. "Information Technology Youth Apprenticeship." Retrieved August 15, 2013 (http://dwd .wisconsin.gov/dwd/publications/dws/ youthapprenticeship/detw_13106_p.pdf).

Index

A

Academies of Information Technology (AOIT), 36
Academy of Information Technology and Robotics (AITR), 35–36
accreditation agencies, 24–25, 48
Apple, 45
apprenticeships, 56–57
apps, 4
associate's degrees, 40, 49, 62

B

bachelor's degrees, 20, 42, 51, 62

C

CanLearn, 52
career academies, 33–37
Career Connection Cadre, 36
career shadowing, 36
certification, 4, 6, 26, 29, 32, 39, 40, 42–45, 48, 49
clubs, 23, 29
community colleges, 6, 29, 39–42, 45, 49, 60
competitions, 23, 29
Computer Learning Center, 46
computer security, 8, 10, 27, 62
Computing Technology Industry Association (CompTIA), 45
corporate sponsors, 33, 36, 61
counseling, 21–23, 32, 40, 46, 51
CyFair, 27, 29, 30

D

deductive reasoning, 17
disabled students, 54
dual-credit courses, 6, 29, 30–32, 40

E

Edgerton, Edward, 14
Electronics Technicians Association (ETA), 45
e-mail, 8, 15, 17, 18

F

FAFSA forms, 52
Federal Perkins Loan Program, 55–56
field studies, 36
financial aid, 6, 23, 28, 51–56, 60
for-profit schools, 49, 60, 62
four-year colleges, 4, 20, 34, 41, 51

G

gaming, 10, 36
Government Accountability Office (GAO), 49

government assistance, 6, 52
graduate degrees, 4, 51
grants, 24, 49, 51, 52, 53–54

H

hackers, 10, 27
hardware, 7, 8, 10, 14, 15, 20, 27, 36, 45, 57
Harvard University, 37, 61
help desks, 13, 15–16, 17, 62
high school diplomas, 39
High Schools That Work, 37
How to Earn Nothing and Learn Little in the Brave New Economy, 58

I

IBM, 32
Information Technology Association of America (ITAA), 7
insurance companies, 62
interest groups, 23
Internet service providers, 7, 15
internships, 6, 23, 24, 28, 36, 37, 51, 57–58, 60, 61
IT technician, career as a,
  getting started, 17–25
  life and times of, 7–16
  other considerations, 51–65
  overview, 4–6
  post-high school, 39–50
  salaries, 24, 40, 49
  specialized training, 26–38
ITT Tech, 60, 62

J

job interviews, 36, 63–64

L

Linked Learning Initiative, 37
loans, 24, 49, 51, 53, 54–56, 62
Lone Star College System, 30, 44

M

Mahaney, Ted, 46
malware, 10, 27
Mann, Josh, 60, 62–63
mentoring, 33, 36, 37, 46
minorities, 36, 54
Microsoft, 29, 32, 45, 46

N

National Academy Foundation (NAF), 36, 37
net price calculators, 48
networking, 4, 7, 10, 13, 14, 15, 20, 27, 33, 46, 62
nonprofit organizations, 45, 57, 58, 61
Novell, 46

O

Occupational Outlook Handbook, 24
O*NET, 4, 24

online courses, 39, 44, 48, 50
online resources, 24–25
operating systems, 27

P

part-time jobs, 28, 57
"Pathways to Prosperity" report, 37, 61
PCs, 36
peer tutoring programs, 29
Perlin, Ross, 57–58
printers, 13, 20
P-Tech, 32–33
publishing companies, 15

R

rebooting, 18
recruiters, 49
résumés, 28, 29, 36, 65
retail companies, 14
robotics, 36

S

scholarships, 52, 53, 54, 60
Scouting, 60
software, 6, 7, 8, 10, 14, 15, 27, 36, 45, 57
Southern Regional Education Board, 37
stipends, 61
student-business connections, 37, 61

T

telephone interviews, 63–64
Tennessee Technology Centers (TTC), 48, 50
troubleshooting, 13, 20, 27

U

U.S. Congress, 49, 55
U.S. Department of Education, 24, 52, 54, 57
U.S. Department of Labor, 24, 54

V

viruses, 10, 27
volunteering, 28, 29

W

webinars, 24
Whalen, Mike, 15–16
Windows, 46
Wisconsin Youth Apprenticeship (YA) program, 56–57
word processing, 10, 17
work-study programs, 6, 22, 25, 51, 56, 57

Y

Year Up, 61

About the Author

Writer and educator Terry Teague Meyer lives in Houston, Texas. She has written a previous book on preparing for a career in digital forensics. Having had to call or e-mail computer support people on many occasions, she has great respect for their expertise and patience.

Photo Credits

Cover (figure) JCREATION/Shutterstock.com; cover (background), pp. 1, 3 XAOC/Shutterstock.com; p. 5 Purestock/Thinkstock; pp. 8–9, 16 Bloomberg/Getty Images; p. 11 AFP/Getty Images; pp. 12–13 Google/AP Images; pp. 18–19 Jupiterimages/Pixland/Thinkstock; pp. 21, 22, 30, 58–59 © AP Images; p. 28 Paul Vasarhelyi/iStock/Thinkstock; p. 31 © Wang Lei/Xinhua/ZUMA Press; pp. 34–35 © Taylor Jones/The Palm Beach Post/ZUMA Press; pp. 40–41 Melanie Stetson Freeman/The Christian Science Monitor/AP Images; p. 43 © Tampa Bay Times/ZUMA Press; p. 47 Tariq Zehawi/MCT/Landov; p. 55 Nigel Carse/E+/Getty Images; p. 64 monkeybusinessimages/iStock/Thinkstock; cover and interior elements isak55/Shutterstock.com (program code), Jirsak/Shutterstock.com (tablet frame), schab/Shutterstock.com (text highlighting), nikifiva/Shutterstock.com (stripe textures), Zfoto/Shutterstock.com (abstract curves); back cover graphics sramcreations/Shutterstock.com; musicman/Shutterstock.com (laptop icon).

Designer: Michael Moy; Editor: Jeanne Nagle; Photo Researcher: Amy Feinberg